Pooh Goes Visiting

From the stories by A. A. Milne

Winnie the Pooh is walking through the Forest one day. He is humming a song to himself.

Suddenly he comes to a hole. "That hole is where Rabbit lives," says Pooh. "I wonder if he has anything for me to eat?"

"Is anybody there?"
Pooh calls.
There is no answer.
"Bother!" says Pooh.

Pooh tries again. "Rabbit, are
you there?" he says. "It's me,
Pooh Bear!"
"Are you sure?" says Rabbit.

"Quite, quite sure,"
says Pooh.
"Oh well, come in,"
says Rabbit.

Pooh pushes and
pushes his way
through the hole.
By now he is very hungry
for some elevenses.
Rabbit fetches some
bread and honey
for Pooh.
When he has
eaten everything,
Pooh says in a
sticky voice that
he'd better be on
his way.

Pooh starts to climb
out of the hole.
Soon his nose is out
in the open ...
then his ears ...
and then his front paws ...
and then his shoulders ...
and then —
"Oh, help!" says Pooh. "I can't
get out! Oh, bother!"

"Are you stuck?" asks Rabbit. He takes Pooh's paw and tries to pull him out. "Ow!" cries Pooh. "That hurts!" "It all comes of eating too much," says Rabbit. "I'll go and find Christopher Robin."

"Silly old Bear," says
Christopher Robin. "Now
we'll have to wait for you to
get thin again."
Pooh is rather anxious. It
could take a week for him
to get thin again.

Christopher Robin says Pooh
can't have any meals, but
that he will read to him
instead.

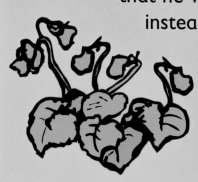

So Christopher Robin reads
to Pooh Bear. Pooh can feel
himself getting thinner and
thinner. And at the end of
the week, Christopher Robin
says, "Now!"

He takes hold of Pooh's front paws.
Rabbit takes hold of Christopher
Robin. All Rabbit's friends and
relations take hold of Rabbit, and
they all pull together ...
For a long time Pooh
says, "Ow!" ...
and, "Oh!" ...

And then, suddenly, "Pop!"
They all fall over backwards ... and
on top of them comes
Winnie-the-Pooh!

"Thank you," says Pooh.
He sets off on his walk ...
"Silly Old Bear!" says
Christopher Robin lovingly.